The Fi...

and other silly stories

Compiled by Vic Parker

Miles

First published in 2013 by Miles Kelly Publishing Ltd
Harding's Barn, Bardfield End Green, Thaxted, Essex, CM6 3PX, UK

2 4 6 8 10 9 7 5 3 1

Publishing Director Belinda Gallagher
Creative Director Jo Cowan
Editorial Director Rosie McGuire
Senior Editor Carly Blake
Editorial Assistant Amy Johnson
Designer Joe Jones
Production Manager Elizabeth Collins
Reprographics Stephan Davis, Jennifer Hunt, Thom Allaway

ISBN 978-1-84810-928-5

Printed in China

British Library Cataloging-in-Publication Data
A catalog record for this book is available from the British Library

ACKNOWLEDGMENTS
The publishers would like to thank the following artists who have contributed to this book:
Beehive Illustration Agency: Mike Phillips
The Bright Agency: Michael Garton (inc. cover)
Jan Lewis, Aimee Mappley (decorative frames)

All other artwork from the Miles Kelly Artwork Bank

Made with paper from a sustainable forest

www.mileskelly.net info@mileskelly.net

www.factsforprojects.com

Contents

Which was the Foolishest?

By Andrew Lang

In a little village that stood on a wide plain, where you could see the sun from the moment he rose to the moment he set, there lived two couples side by side. The men, who both worked under the same master, were good friends, but their wives were always arguing, and the subject they argued most about was which of the two had the stupidest husband. Each woman thought

her own husband the more foolish.

"You should just see what he does!" one woman said to her neighbor. "When he dresses the baby, he puts her dress on upside down, and, one day, I found him trying to feed her with boiling hot soup. Then he picks up stones in the road and sows them instead of potatoes, and one day he wanted to go into the garden from the top window, because he thought it was a shorter way than through the door."

"That is bad enough, of course," answered the other woman, "but it is really nothing to what I have to endure every day from my husband. If, when I am busy, I ask him to go and feed the hens, he is certain to give them some poisonous stuff instead of their proper food, and when I visit the yard next I find them all dead. Once, when I had gone away to my sick mother, he took my best hat, and when I came back I found he had given it to the hen to lay her eggs in. And you know that, only last week, when I sent him to buy butter he returned driving a hundred and fifty ducks that someone had persuaded him to take. And not one of them would lay!"

"Yes, I am afraid he is trying," replied the first woman, "but let us put them to the test, and see which of them is the most foolish."

So, about the time that she expected her husband home from work, the first wife got out her spinning-wheel, and sat busily turning it, taking care not even to look up from her work when the man came in. For some minutes he stood with his mouth open watching her, and as she still remained silent, he said at last, "Have you gone mad, wife, that you sit spinning without anything on the wheel?"

"You may think that there is nothing on it," answered she, "but I can assure you that there is a large skein of wool, so fine that you can't see it, which will be woven into a coat for you."

"Dear me!" he

replied. "What a clever wife I have got! If you had not told me I should never have known that there was any wool on the wheel at all. But now I really do seem to see something."

The woman smiled and after spinning for an hour more, she began to weave as fast as she could. At last she said to her husband, "I am too tired to finish it tonight, so I shall go to bed. Tomorrow I shall only have the cutting and stitching to do."

So the next morning she got up early, and the sound of her scissors could be heard *snip! snap!* as far as the garden. Her husband could not see anything to snip at, but he was so stupid that this was not surprising!

After the cutting came the sewing. Then

she turned to her husband and said, "Now it is ready for you to try on." She made him take off his coat and stand up in front of her. Then, once more, she patted and pinned and fixed and joined, and was very careful in smoothing out every wrinkle.

"It does not feel very warm," observed the man at last.

"That is because it is so fine," answered she, "you do not want it to be as thick as the rough clothes you wear every day."

He did but was ashamed to say so, and only answered, "Well, I am sure it must be beautiful since you say so, and I shall be smarter than anyone in the village. 'Oh, what a splendid coat!' they will exclaim when they see me. But it is not everybody who has a wife as clever as mine."

Meanwhile, the other wife was not idle. As soon as her husband entered she stared at him with such a look of terror that the poor man was quite frightened.

"Why do you stare at me so? Is there anything the matter?" he asked.

"Oh! Go to bed at once," she cried. "You must be very ill indeed to look like that!"

The man was surprised at first, as he felt particularly well that evening, but the moment his wife spoke he became certain that he had something the matter with him.

"I dare say it would be the best place for me," he answered, trembling, and he asked his wife to take him upstairs and help him change into his night clothes.

"If you sleep well during the night there may be a chance for you," said she, as she tucked him up warmly, "but if not…"

Of course the poor man never closed an eye till the sun rose.

"How do you feel this morning?" asked the woman, coming in quietly.

"Oh very bad indeed," said he. "Can you think of nothing to make me better?"

"I will try everything that is possible," said the wife, who did not in the least wish her husband to die, but was determined to show that he was more foolish than the other man. "I will get some herbs and make you a drink, but I am very afraid that it is too late. Why did you not tell me before?"

"I thought perhaps the pain would go off in a day or two, and besides, I did not want to make you unhappy," answered the man. "Of course, if I had had any idea how ill I really was, I would have spoken at once."

"Well, well, I will see what can be done," said the wife, "but talking is not good for you. Lie still and keep yourself warm."

All that day the man lay in bed, and whenever his wife entered the room and asked how he felt, he replied that he was getting worse. In the evening, she burst into tears, and sobbed, "Oh, my husband, are you really dead? I must order your coffin."

Now, when the man heard this all at once he knew that he was as well as ever.

"Oh, no, no!" he cried. "I feel quite recovered! I think I shall go out to work."

"You will do no such thing," replied his wife. "Just keep quite quiet, for before the sun rises you will be dead."

The man was frightened at her words, and lay absolutely still while the undertaker came and measured him for his coffin.

That evening the coffin was sent to their home. In the morning the woman dressed her husband and called the undertaker's men to fasten the lid and carry him to the grave, where all their friends were waiting.

Just as the body was being placed in the ground the other woman's husband came running up, dressed in no clothes at all. Everybody burst into shouts of laughter at the sight, and the men laid down the coffin and laughed too, till their sides nearly split. The dead man was so astonished at this that he peeped out of a little window in the side of the coffin, and cried out, "I should

laugh as loudly as any of you, if I were not a dead man."

When they heard the voice from the coffin, the people stopped laughing and rushed to lift the lid.

"Were you really not dead?" asked they. "And if not, why did you let yourself be buried?"

The wives confessed that they had each wished to prove that her husband was stupider. But the villagers could not decide which was the most foolish.

So the women argued just as before, and no one knew whose husband was the most foolish.

The Fish and the Hare

By Andrew Lang

Once upon a time an old man and his wife lived together in a little village. One day, the old man was walking in a forest when his foot sank into some newly turned earth. Curious, he dug and dug, and at last he uncovered a pot full of gold and silver.

'Oh, what luck!' he thought. 'But I can't take it home because my wife is a terrible gossip – she'll tell the whole world!'

He thought hard and made a plan. He covered up the pot again with earth and went to market, where he bought a live fish and a live hare. Then he hurried back to the forest and hung the fish up at the top of a tree and tied up the hare at the edge of a stream. Then he trotted merrily home.

"Wife!" he cried. "I've found a pot full of treasure! Come with me and we'll fetch it."

On the way, the man said, "What strange things one hears, wife! I was told only the other day that fish now live in the treetops and some wild animals spend their time in the water. Times are changed."

"What nonsense people talk," replied she. Of course, it wasn't long before the

The Fish and the Hare

couple came across the fish flapping at the top of the tree and the hare wriggling in the water – and the wife was shocked. Lost for words, the man drove his wife to where the treasure was buried, and they dug up the pot and drove home again.

So now the old couple had plenty of money. But the wife was foolish, and every day she asked lots of people to dinner and laid on huge feasts. Her husband grew cross that she was spending away their fortune.

The woman just went straight off to the mayor to complain.

"Oh, my lord!" she moaned. "Ever since my husband found the treasure there is no bearing him. He won't work, and keeps all the money to himself."

The mayor took pity on the woman, and ordered his secretary to go to the man's house and take the treasure for safekeeping.

But the old man just shrugged his shoulders and said, "What treasure? Pardon me, Your Excellency, but my wife must have imagined it, sir. Ask her how it happened."

"Well, Mr. Secretary," cried the wife, "we were driving through the forest, and we saw a fish at home in the top of a tree and a hare living in the stream—"

"What! Are you making fun of me?" shouted the secretary, losing his temper.

After that the old woman had to hold her tongue, and the man spent part of the treasure in opening a shop. He prospered and spent the rest of his days in peace.

The Endless Tale

By James Baldwin

Once upon a time in the Far East there was a great King. Every day and all day long, he sat on cushions and listened to stories. No matter what the story was about, he never grew tired of hearing it, no matter how long it was.

"There is only one fault that I find with your story," he often said to the storyteller, "it is too short."

Eventually the King had an idea. He sent out a proclamation saying that the greatest storytellers in the world were invited to his palace. From far and wide they arrived, and some of them told tales that were very long indeed. But the King was always sad when a story came to an end.

At last he sent word into every city and town and country place, offering a prize to anyone who should tell him a tale that had no end at all. He said, "To the man that will tell me a story which shall last forever, I will give my fairest daughter for his wife, and I will make him my heir."

But he added a very hard condition. "If any man shall try to tell such a story and then fail, he shall have his head cut off."

The King's daughter was very pretty, and there were many young men in that country who were willing to do anything to win her. But none of them wanted to lose their heads, so only a few tried for the prize.

One brave young man invented a story that lasted three months, but at the end of that time he could think of nothing more. His fate was a warning to others, and it was a long time before another storyteller was brave enough to try the King's patience.

But one day a stranger from the South came into the palace. "Great King," he said, "is it true that you offer a prize to the man who can tell a story that has no end?"

"It is true," said the King.

"And shall this man have your fairest

daughter for his wife? Will he be your heir?"

"Yes, if he succeeds," said the King. "But if he fails, he shall lose his head."

"Very well, then," said the stranger. "I have a pleasant story about locusts to tell."

"Locusts?" remarked the King, his eyes gleaming with delight. "No one has ever told me a tale about locusts before. Do tell it," said the King. "I will gladly listen."

The storyteller began his tale.

"Once upon a time a king seized all the wheat in his country, and stored it away in a strong granary. But a swarm of hungry locusts came over the land and saw where the grain had been put. After searching for many days they found on the east side of the granary a tiny crack that was just large enough for one locust to pass through at a time. So one locust went in and carried away a grain of wheat, then another locust went in and carried away a grain of wheat, then another locust went in and carried away a grain of wheat..."

Day after day, week after week, the man kept on saying, "Then another locust went in and carried away a grain of wheat..."

A month passed, a year passed, and still the man

kept on saying, "Then another locust went in and carried away a grain of wheat…" At the end of two years, the King said, "How much longer will the locusts be going in and carrying away wheat?"

"O King," said the storyteller, "they have as yet cleared only one cubit, and there are many thousand cubits in the granary."

"You will drive me mad!" cried the King. "I can listen no longer. Take my daughter, rule my kingdom. But do not let me hear another word about those horrible locusts!"

And so the storyteller married the King's daughter, and he lived happily in the land. But his father-in-law, the King, did not care to listen to any more stories.

How Mr. Rabbit Lost His Tail

By Albert Bigelow Paine

"Once upon a time," said Mr. Rabbit at storytime, "a great many great-grandfathers back, my family had long bushy tails like Mr. Squirrel and Mr. Fox, only a good deal longer and finer, and very handsome."

When Mr. Rabbit said that, Mr. Squirrel sniffed and twitched his nose and gave his nice bushy tail a flirt, but he didn't say anything. Mr. Rabbit went right on.

"Well, there was one fine, handsome rabbit who had the longest and plumiest tail of any of the family and was very proud of it. He was my twenty-seventh great-grandfather and was called Mr. Hare. He was young and smart then, and thought he was a good deal smarter than he really was, though he was smart and handsome enough to set the style for the other rabbits. Not much ever really happened to him, because he could beat anything running that there was in the Big Deep Woods.

"That twenty-seventh great-grandfather of mine was very proud of his running, and used to brag that in a foot race he could beat anything that lived between the Wide Grass Lands and the edge of the world. He used to talk about it to almost everybody that came along. One day he met one of the Turtle family, who used to be called Mr. Tortoise in those days. He stopped and began to brag to Mr. Tortoise how fast he could run and how nobody in the Big Deep Woods dared to race with him.

"But Mr. Tortoise just smiled a little and said, 'Oh, pshaw! You can't run very fast. I believe I can beat you myself!'

"Well, that did make Grandpaw Hare laugh – and made him a little mad, too. 'You!' he said. 'Why, I'll give you within ten yards of that rail fence half a mile away, and then beat you across it. Just travel along, and some time this afternoon when you get down that way, I'll come back and let you see me go by. But you'll have to look quick, for I'll be going fast.'

"But Mr. Tortoise said he didn't want any start at all, that he was ready to begin the race right then. That made Grandpaw Hare laugh so loud that Mr. Fox heard him as he was passing, and came over to see what the fun was. Mr. Fox said that he hadn't much to do, and that he'd stay and act as judge. He thought a race like that wouldn't last long – and it didn't, though it wasn't at all the kind of a race he had expected.

"Well, he put Mr. Tortoise and my twenty-seventh great-grandfather side by side, and then he stood off and said, 'Go!'

He thought it would be over in a minute. "Grandpaw Hare gave one great big leap, about twenty feet long, and then stopped. He wanted to have some fun with Mr. Tortoise. He looked around to where Mr. Tortoise was coming panting along, and he laughed and rolled over to see how solemn he looked. Mr. Tortoise was down on all fours so he could use all his legs at once, and anybody would think that he expected to win the race.

"The more my Grandpaw Hare looked at him the more he laughed. Then he would make another long leap forward and stop, and wait for Mr. Tortoise to catch up again.

"Then he would call to him, or maybe go back, and say, 'Come along there, old tobacco box. Are you tied to something?' Mr. Fox told my ancestor to go on and finish the race – that he couldn't wait around there all day. Pretty soon Mr. Fox said if they were going to fool along like that, he'd just go down to the fence and take a nap till they got there.

"Mr. Fox loped away to the fence, and laid down and went to sleep in the shade. Grandpaw Hare thought it would be fun to pretend to be asleep, too. I've heard a story told about it that says that he really did go to sleep, and that Mr. Tortoise went by him and got to the fence before he woke up. But that is not the way it happened. My twenty-seventh great-grandfather was too smart to go to sleep, and even if he had gone to sleep, Mr. Tortoise made enough noise to wake up forty of our family.

"My ancestor would wait until Mr. Tortoise came along and was up even with him, then suddenly he'd sit up as if he'd been woken out of a dream and say, 'Hello! What do you want to wake me up for when I'm trying to get a nap?' Then he would laugh a big laugh and make another leap, and lie down and pretend again.

"But Grandpaw Hare carried the joke a

little too far. He kept letting Mr. Tortoise get up closer and closer every time, until Mr. Tortoise would almost step on him before he would move. And that was what Mr. Tortoise wanted, for the next time he came along he came right up behind my ancestor. Instead of stepping on him, Mr. Tortoise gave his head a quick snap, just as if he were catching fish. He grabbed my Grandpaw Hare by that beautiful plumy tail, and held on. My ancestor gave a squeal

and a holler, and set out for that rail fence, telling his troubles as he came.

"Mr. Fox had gone sound asleep and didn't hear all the noise at first. When he did he thought Grandpaw was just calling to him to wake up and be ready to judge the race, so he sat up quick and watched them come. He saw my twenty-seventh great-grandfather sailing along, with something that looked like an old rusty old pan tied to his tail.

"When Mr. Fox saw what it was, he just laid down, and laughed, and then hopped up on the top rail and called out, 'All right, I'm awake, Mr. Hare! Come right along, Mr. Hare! You'll beat him yet!'

"Then Mr. Fox saw my ancestor stop

and shake himself, to try to get Mr. Tortoise loose. This he couldn't do, for, as we all know, whenever any of the Turtle family get a grip they never let go till it thunders, and this was a bright day. So pretty soon Grandpaw was up and running again, with Mr. Tortoise sailing behind. Mr. Fox laughed to see them coming, and called out, 'Come right along, Mr. Hare! You'll beat him yet!'

"But Mr. Fox made a mistake about that. Grandpaw Hare was ahead, of course, but when he got close to the fence he made one more try to get Mr. Tortoise loose. He gave his tail a great big swing. But Mr. Tortoise didn't let go quite quick enough, and off came my twenty-seventh great-grandfather's beautiful plumy tail,

and away went Mr. Tortoise with it, clear over the top rail of the fence, and landed in a brier patch on the other side.

"Well, Grandpaw Hare was in such a state as you never heard of! He forgot all about the race, and just raved about his loss.

Grandpaw Hare said that he never in the world could show his face again.

"Mr. Fox stopped laughing as soon as he could, and was really quite sorry for him. Even Mr. Tortoise looked through the fence, and asked him if he didn't think it could be spliced and be almost as good as ever.

"He said he hadn't meant to commit any injury, and that he hoped Mr. Hare would live to forgive him, and there was no reason why my grandpaw shouldn't beat him in the next race.

"Then my ancestor remembered about the

race and forgot his other loss for a minute. He declared that Mr. Tortoise didn't win the race at all – that he couldn't have covered that much ground in half a day alone. He asked Mr. Fox if he was going to let that great straddle bug ruin his reputation for speed, besides all the other damage he had done.

"Then Mr. Fox scratched his head, and thought. He said he didn't see how he could help giving the race to Mr. Tortoise, for it was to be the first one across the fence, and Mr. Tortoise was certainly the first one across, and he'd gone over the top in style.

"Well, that made Grandpaw Hare madder than ever. He didn't say another word, but just picked up his property that Mr. Tortoise handed him, and set off by a back way. He was thinking what he ought to do to keep everybody from laughing at him. He had always been so proud that if people laughed he knew he could never show his face again.

"And that," said Mr. Rabbit, "is the true story of that old race between the hare and the tortoise, and of how the first rabbit came to lose his tail."